JULIAN BARNES

---

EVERMORE

PICTURES BY HOWARD HODGKIN

PENGUIN BOOKS

PENGUIN BOOKS

Published by the Penguin Group
Penguin Books Ltd, 27 Wrights Lane, London w8 5TZ, England
Penguin Books USA Inc., 375 Hudson Street, New York, New York 10014, USA
Penguin Books Australia Ltd, Ringwood, Victoria, Australia
Penguin Books Canada Ltd, 10 Alcorn Avenue, Toronto, Ontario, Canada M4V 3B2
Penguin Books (NZ) Ltd, 182 – 190 Wairau Road, Auckland 10, New Zealand

Penguin Books Ltd, Registered Offices: Harmondsworth, Middlesex, England

First published by Cape in *Cross Channel* 1996

Published in Penguin Books 1996
1 3 5 7 9 10 8 6 4 2

Set in 11.5/16pt Monotype Bembo
Typeset by Rowland Phototypesetting Ltd, Bury St Edmunds, Suffolk
Printed in England by Clays Ltd, St Ives plc

Julian Barnes was born in Leicester in 1946. His books include *Metroland*, which won the 1981 Somerset Maugham Award; *Flaubert's Parrot*, winner of the 1986 Prix Médicis; *Staring at the Sun*; *A History of the World in 10½ Chapters*; *Talking it Over*, which won the Prix Fémina in 1992; and *Cross Channel*, in which *Evermore* originally appeared.

The painter Howard Hodgkin was born in 1932. He represented Britain at the 1984 Venice Biennale and won the Turner Prize the following year. His recent exhibition at the Metropolitan Museum of Art, New York, *Howard Hodgkin: Paintings 1975−1995*, will be shown in London this winter at the Hayward Gallery.

All the time she carried them with her, in a bag knotted at the neck. She had bayoneted the polythene with a fork, so that condensation would not gather and begin to rot the frail card. She knew what happened when you covered seedlings in a flower-pot: damp came from nowhere to make its sudden climate. This had to be avoided. There had been so much wet back then, so much rain, churned mud and drowned horses. She did not mind it for herself. She minded it for them still, for all of them, back then.

There were three postcards, the last he had sent. The earlier ones had been divided up, lost perhaps, but she had the last of them, his final evidence. On the day itself, she would unknot the bag and trace her eyes over the jerky pencilled address, the formal signature (initials and surname only), the obedient crossings-out. For many years she had ached at what the cards did not say; but nowadays she found something in their official impassivity which seemed proper, even if not consoling.

Of course she did not need actually to look at them, any more than she needed the photograph to recall his dark eyes, sticky-out ears, and the jaunty smile which agreed that the fun would be all over by Christmas. At any moment she could bring the three pieces of buff field-service card exactly to mind. The dates: Dec 24, Jan 11, Jan 17, written in his own hand, and confirmed by the postmark which added the years: 16, 17, 17. 'NOTHING is to be written on this side except the date and signature of the sender. Sentences not required may be erased. <u>If anything else is added the postcard will be destroyed</u>.' And then the brutal choices.

```
I am quite well
I am being admitted into hospital
    ⎧ sick    ⎫ and am going on well
    ⎩ wounded ⎭ and hope to be discharged soon
I am being sent down to the base
                       ⎧ letter dated . . . . . . . . .
I have received your  ⎨ telegram . . . . . . . . . . .
                       ⎩ parcel . . . . . . . . . . . . .
Letter follows at first opportunity
I have received no letter from you
    ⎧ Lately
    ⎩ For a long time
```

He was quite well on each occasion. He had never been admitted into hospital. He was not being sent down to the base. He had received a letter of a certain date. A letter would follow at the first opportunity. He had not received no letter. All done with thick pencilled crossing-out and a single date. Then, beside the instruction <u>Signature only</u>, the last signal from her brother. S. Moss. A large looping S with a circling full stop after it. Then Moss written without lifting from the card what she always imagined as a stub of pencil-end studiously licked.

On the other side, their mother's name – Mrs Moss, with a grand M and a short stabbing line beneath the *rs* – then the address. Another warning down the edge, this time in smaller letters. 'The address only to be written on this side. If anything else is added, the postcard will be destroyed.' But across the top of her second card, Sammy had written something, and it had not been destroyed. A neat line of ink without the rough loopiness of his pencilled signature: '50 yds from the Germans. Posted from Trench.' In fifty years, one for each underlined yard, she had not come up with the answer. Why had he written it, why in ink, why had they allowed it? Sam was a cautious and responsible boy, especially towards their mother, and he would not have risked a worrying silence. But he had undeniably written these words. And in ink, too. Was it code for something else? A premonition of death? Except that Sam was not the sort to have premonitions. Perhaps it was simply excitement, a desire to impress. Look how close we are. 50 yds from the Germans. Posted from Trench.

She was glad he was at Cabaret Rouge, with his own headstone. Found and identified. Given known and honoured burial. She had a horror of Thiepval, one which failed to diminish in spite of her dutiful yearly visits. Thiepval's lost souls.

You had to make the right preparation for them, for their lostness. So she always began elsewhere, at Caterpillar Valley, Thistle Dump, Quarry, Blighty Valley, Ulster Tower, Herbécourt.

> No Morning Dawns
> No Night Returns
> But What We Think Of Thee

That was at Herbécourt, a walled enclosure in the middle of fields, room for a couple of hundred, most of them Australian, but this was a British lad, the one who owned this inscription. Was it a vice to have become such a connoisseur of grief? Yet it was true, she had her favourite cemeteries. Like Blighty Valley and Thistle Dump, both half-hidden from the road in a fold of valley; or Quarry, a graveyard looking as if it had been abandoned by its village; or Devonshire, that tiny, private patch for the Devonshires who died on the first day of the Somme, who fought to hold that ridge and held it still. You followed signposts in British racing green, then walked across fields guarded by wooden martyred Christs to these sanctuaries of orderliness, where everything was accounted for. Headstones were lined up like dominoes on edge; beneath them, their owners were present and correct, listed, tended. Creamy altars proclaimed that THEIR NAME LIVETH FOR EVERMORE. And so it did, on the graves, in the books, in hearts, in memories.

Each year she wondered if this would be her last visit. Her life no longer offered up to her the confident plausibility of two decades more, one decade, five years. Instead, it was now renewed on an annual basis, like her driving licence. Every April Dr Holling had to certify her fit for another twelve months behind the wheel. Perhaps she and the Morris would go kaput on the same day.

Before, it had been the boat train, the express to Amiens, a local stopper, a bus or two. Since she had acquired the Morris, she had in theory become freer; and yet her routine remained almost immutable. She would drive to Dover and take a night ferry, riding the Channel in the blackout alongside burly lorry-drivers. It saved money, and meant she was always in France for daybreak. No Morning Dawns . . . He must have seen each daybreak and wondered if that was the date they would put on his stone . . . Then she would follow the N43 to St-Omer, to Aire and Lillers, where she usually took a croissant and *thé à l'anglaise*. From Lillers the N43 continued to Béthune, but she flinched from it: south of Béthune was the D937 to Arras, and there, on a straight stretch where the road did a reminding elbow, was Brigadier Sir Frank Higginson's domed portico. You should not drive past it, even if you intended to return. She had done that once, early in her ownership of the Morris, skirted Cabaret Rouge in second gear, and it had seemed the grossest discourtesy to Sammy and those who lay beside him: no, it's not your turn yet, just you wait and we'll be along. No, that was what the other motorists did.

So instead she would cut south from Lillers and come into Arras with the D341. From there, in that thinned triangle whose southern points were Albert and Péronne, she would begin her solemn and necessary tour of the woods and fields in which, so many decades before, the British Army had counter-attacked to relieve the pressure on the French at Verdun. That had been the start of it, anyway. No doubt scholars were by now having second thoughts, but that was what they were for; she herself no longer had arguments to deploy or positions to hold. She valued only what she had experienced at the time: an outline of strategy, the conviction of gallantry, and the facts of mourning.

At first, back then, the commonality of grief had helped: wives, mothers, comrades, an array of brass hats, and a bugler amid gassy morning mist which the feeble November sun had failed to burn away. Later, remembering Sam had changed: it became work, continuity; instead of anguish and glory, there was fierce unreasonableness, both about his death and her commemoration of it. During this period, she was hungry for the solitude and the voluptuous selfishness of grief: her Sam, her loss, her mourning, and nobody else's similar. She admitted as much: there was no shame to it. But now, after half a century, her feelings had simply become part of her. Her grief was a calliper, necessary and supporting; she could not imagine walking without it.

When she had finished with Herbécourt and Devonshire, Thistle Dump and Caterpillar Valley, she would come, always with trepidation, to the great red-brick memorial at Thiepval. An arch of triumph, yes, but of what kind, she wondered: the triumph over death, or the triumph *of* death? 'Here are recorded names of officers and men of the British armies who fell on the Somme battlefields July 1915–February 1918 but to whom the fortune of war denied the known and honoured burial given to their comrades in death.' Thiepval Ridge, Pozières Wood, Albert, Morval, Ginchy, Guillemont, Ancre, Ancre Heights, High Wood, Delville Wood, Bapaume, Bazentin Ridge, Miraumont, Transloy Ridges, Flers-Courcelette. Battle after battle, each accorded its stone laurel wreath, its section of wall: name after name after name, the Missing of the Somme, the official graffiti of death. This monument by Sir Edwin Lutyens revolted her, it always had. She could not bear the thought of these lost men, exploded into unrecognizable pieces, engulfed in the mud-fields, one moment fully there with pack and gaiters, baccy and rations, with their memories and their hopes, their past and their future, crammed into them, and the next moment only a shred of khaki or a sliver of shin-bone to prove they had ever existed. Or worse: some of these names had first been given known and honoured burial, their allotment of ground with their name above it, only for some new battle with its heedless artillery to tear up the temporary graveyard and bring a second, final extermination. Yet each of those scraps of uniform and flesh – whether newly killed or richly decomposed – had been brought back here and reorganized, conscripted into the eternal regiment of the missing, kitted out and made to dress by the right. Something about the way they had vanished and the way they were now reclaimed was more than she could bear: as if an army which had thrown them away so lightly now chose to own them again so gravely. She was not sure whether this was the case. She claimed no understanding of military matters. All she claimed was an understanding of grief.

Her wariness of Thiepval always made her read it with a sceptical, a proof-reader's eye. She noticed, for instance, that the French translation of the English inscription listed – as the English one did not – the exact number of the Missing. 73,367. That was another reason she did not care to be here, standing in the middle of the arch looking down over the puny Anglo-French cemetery (French crosses to the left, British stones to the right) while the wind drew tears from an averting eye. 73,367: beyond a certain point, the numbers became uncountable and diminishing in effect. The more dead, the less proportionate the pain. 73,367: even she, with all her expertise in grief, could not imagine that.

Perhaps the British realized that the number of the Missing might continue to grow through the years, that no fixed total could be true; perhaps it was not shame, but a kind of sensible poetry which made them decline to specify a figure. And they were right: the numbers had indeed changed. The arch was inaugurated in 1932 by the Prince of Wales, and all the names of all the Missing had been carved upon its surfaces, but still, here and there, out of their proper place, hauled back tardily from oblivion, were a few soldiers enlisted only under the heading of Addenda. She knew all their names by now:

Dodds T., Northumberland Fusiliers; Malcolm H. W., The Cameronians; Lennox F. J., Royal Irish Rifles; Lovell F. H. B., Royal Warwickshire Regiment; Orr R., Royal Inniskillins; Forbes R., Cameron Highlanders; Roberts J., Middlesex Regiment; Moxham A., Wiltshire Regiment; Humphries F. J., Middlesex Regiment; Hughes H. W., Worcestershire Regiment; Bateman W. T., Northamptonshire Regiment; Tarling E., The Cameronians; Richards W., Royal Field Artillery; Rollins S., East Lancashire Regiment; Byrne L., Royal Irish Rifles; Gale E. O., East Yorkshire Regiment; Walters J., Royal Fusiliers; Argar D., Royal Field Artillery. No Morning Dawns, No Night Returns . . .

She felt closest to Rollins S., since he was an East Lancashire; she would always smile at the initials inflicted upon Private Lovell; but it was Malcolm H. W. who used to intrigue her most.

Malcolm H. W., or, to give him his full inscription: 'Malcolm H. W. The Cameronians (Sco. Rif.) served as Wilson H.' An addendum and a corrigendum all in one. When she had first discovered him, it had pleased her to imagine his story. Was he under age? Did he falsify his name to escape home, to run away from some girl? Was he wanted for a crime, like those fellows who joined the French Foreign Legion? She did not really want an answer, but she liked to dream a little about this man who had first been deprived of his identity and then of his life. These accumulations of loss seemed to exalt him; for a while, faceless and iconic, he had threatened to rival Sammy and Denis as an emblem of the war. In later years she turned against such fancifulness. There was no mystery really. Private H. W. Malcolm becomes H. Wilson. No doubt he was in truth H. Wilson Malcolm, and when he volunteered they wrote the wrong name in the wrong column; then they were unable to change it. That would make sense: man is only a clerical error corrected by death.

She had never cared for the main inscription over the central arch:

AUX ARMEES
FRANCAISE ET
BRITANNIQUE
L'EMPIRE
BRITANNIQUE
RECON-
NAISSANT

Each line was centred, which was correct, but there was altogether too much white space beneath the inscription. She would have inserted 'less #' on the galley-proof. And each year she disliked more and more the line-break in the word *reconnaissant*. There were different schools of thought about this – she had argued with her superiors over the years – but she insisted that breaking a word in the middle of a doubled consonant was a nonsense. You broke a word where the word itself was perforated. Look what this military, architectural or sculptural nincompoop had produced: a fracture which left a separate word, *naissant*, by mistake. *Naissant* had nothing to do with *reconnaissant*, nothing at all; worse, it introduced the notion of birth on to this monument to death. She had written to the War Graves Commission about it, many years ago, and had been assured that the proper procedures had been followed. They told *her* that!

Nor was she content with EVERMORE.

Their name liveth for evermore: here at Thiepval, also at Cabaret Rouge, Caterpillar Valley, Combles Communal Cemetery Extension, and all the larger memorials. It was of course the correct form, or at least the more regular form; but something in her preferred to see it as two words. EVER MORE: it seemed more weighty like this, with an equal bell-toll on each half. In any case, she had a quarrel with the Dictionary about *evermore*. 'Always, at all times, constantly, continually'. Yes, it could mean this in the ubiquitous inscription. But she preferred sense 1: 'For all future time'. Their name liveth for all future time. No morning dawns, no night returns, but what we think of thee. This is what the inscription meant. But the Dictionary had marked sense 1 as '*Obs. exc. arch.*' Obsolete except archaic. No, oh certainly not, no. And not with a last quotation as recent as 1854. She would have spoken to Mr Rothwell about this, or at least pencilled a looping note on the galley-proof; but this entry was not being revised, and the letter E had passed over her desk without an opportunity to make the adjustment.

EVERMORE. She wondered if there was such a thing as collective memory, something more than the sum of individual memories. If so, was it merely coterminous, yet in some way richer; or did it last longer? She wondered if those too young to have original knowledge could be given memory, could have it grafted on. She thought of this especially at Thiepval. Though she hated the place, when she saw young families trailing across the grass towards the redbrick *arc-de-triomphe* it also roused in her a wary hopefulness. Christian cathedrals could inspire religious faith by their vast assertiveness; why then should not Lutyens' memorial provoke some response equally beyond the rational? That reluctant child, whining about the strange food its mother produced from plastic boxes, might receive memory here. Such an edifice assured the newest eye of the pre-existence of the profoundest emotions. Grief and awe lived here; they could be breathed, absorbed. And if so, then this child might in turn bring its child, and so on, from generation to generation, EVERMORE. Not just to count the Missing, but to understand what those from whom they had gone missing knew, and to feel her loss afresh.

Perhaps this was one reason she had married Denis. Of course she should never have done so. And in a way she never had, for there had been no carnal connection: she unwilling, he incapable. It had lasted two years and his uncomprehending eyes when she delivered him back were impossible to forget. All she could say in her defence was that it was the only time she had behaved with such pure selfishness: she had married him for her own reasons, and discarded him for her own reasons. Some might say that the rest of her life had been selfish too, devoted as it was entirely to her own commemorations; but this was a selfishness that hurt nobody else.

Poor Denis. He was still handsome when he came back, though his hair grew white on one side and he dribbled. When the fits came on she knelt on his chest and held his tongue down with a stub of pencil. Every night he roamed restlessly through his sleep, muttered and roared, fell silent for a while, and then with parade-ground precision would shout *Hip! hip! hip!* When she woke him, he could never remember what had been happening. He had guilt and pain, but no specific memory of what he felt guilty about. She knew: Denis had been hit by shrapnel and taken back down the line to hospital without a farewell to his best pal Jewy Moss, leaving Sammy to be killed during the next day's Hun bombardment. After two years of this marriage, two years of watching Denis vigorously brush his patch of white hair to make it go away, she had returned him to his sisters. From now on, she told them, they should look after Denis and she would look after Sam. The sisters had gazed at her in silent astonishment. Behind them, in the hall, Denis, his chin wet and his brown eyes uncomprehending, stood with an awkward patience which implied that this latest event was nothing special in itself, merely one of a number of things he failed to grasp, and that there would surely be much more to come, all down the rest of his life, which would also escape him.

She had taken the job on the Dictionary a month later. She worked alone in a damp basement, at a desk across which curled long sheets of galley-proof. Condensation beaded the window. She was armed with a brass table-lamp and a pencil which she sharpened until it was too short to fit in the hand. Her script was large and loose, somewhat like Sammy's; she deleted and inserted, just as he had done on his field-service postcards. <u>Nothing to be written on this side of the galley-proof. If anything else is added to the galley-proof it will be destroyed.</u> No, she did not have to worry; she made her marks with impunity. She spotted colons which were italic instead of roman, brackets which were square instead of round, inconsistent abbreviations, misleading cross-references. Occasionally she made suggestions. She might observe, in looping pencil, that such-and-such a word was in her opinion vulgar rather than colloquial, or that the sense illustrated was figurative rather than transferred.

She passed on her galley-proofs to Mr Rothwell, the joint deputy editor, but never enquired whether her annotations were finally acted upon. Mr Rothwell, a bearded, taciturn and pacific man, valued her meticulous eye, her sure grasp of the Dictionary's conventions, and her willingness to take work home if a fascicle was shortly going to press. He remarked to himself and to others that she had a strangely disputatious attitude over words labelled as obsolete. Often she would propose *?Obs.* rather than *Obs.* as the correct marking. Perhaps this had something to do with age, Mr Rothwell thought; younger folk were perhaps more willing to accept that a word had had its day.

In fact, Mr Rothwell was only five years younger than she; but Miss Moss — as she had become once more after her disposal of Denis — had aged quickly, almost as a matter of will. The years passed and she grew stout, her hair flew a little more wildly away from her clips, and her spectacle lenses became thicker. Her stockings had a dense, antique look to them, and she never took her raincoat to the dry-cleaner. Younger lexicographers entering her office, where a number of back files were stored, wondered if the faint smell of rabbit-hutch came from the walls, the old Dictionary slips, Miss Moss's raincoat, or Miss Moss herself. None of this mattered to Mr Rothwell, who saw only the precision of her work. Though entitled by the Press to an annual holiday of fifteen working days, she never took more than a single week.

At first this holiday coincided with the eleventh hour of the eleventh day of the eleventh month; Mr Rothwell had the delicacy not to ask for details. In later years, however, she would take her week in other months, late spring or early autumn. When her parents died and she inherited a small amount of money, she surprised Mr Rothwell by arriving for work one day in a small grey Morris with red leather seats. It sported a yellow metal AA badge on the front and a metal GB plate on the back. At the age of fifty-three she had passed her driving-test first time, and manoeuvred her car with a precision bordering on elan.

She always slept in the car. It saved money; but mainly it helped her be alone with herself and Sam. The villages in that thinned triangle south of Arras became accustomed to the sight of an ageing British car the colour of gunmetal drawn up beside the war memorial; inside, an elderly lady wrapped in a travelling-rug would be asleep in the passenger seat. She never locked the car at night, for it seemed impertinent, even disrespectful on her part to feel any fear. She slept while the villages slept, and would wake as a drenched cow on its way to milking softly shouldered a wing of the parked Morris. Every so often she would be invited in by a villager, but she preferred not to accept hospitality. Her behaviour was not regarded as peculiar, and cafés in the region knew to serve her *thé à l'anglaise* without her having to ask.

After she had finished with Thiepval, with Thistle Dump and Caterpillar Valley, she would drive up through Arras and take the D937 towards Béthune. Ahead lay Vimy, Cabaret Rouge, N.D. de Lorette. But there was always one other visit to be paid first: to Maison Blanche. Such peaceful names they mostly had. But here at Maison Blanche were 40,000 German dead, 40,000 Huns laid out beneath their thin black crosses, a sight as orderly as you would expect from the Huns, though not as splendid as the

British graves. She lingered there, reading a few names at random, idly wondering, when she found a date just a little later than the 21st January 1917, if this could be the Hun that had killed her Sammy. Was this the man who squeezed the trigger, fed the machine-gun, blocked his ears as the howitzer roared? And see how short a time he had lasted afterwards: two days, a week, a month or so in the mud before being lined up in known and honoured burial, facing out once more towards her Sammy, though separated now not by barbed-wire and <u>50 yds</u> but by a few kilometres of asphalt.

She felt no rancour towards these Huns; time had washed from her any anger at the man, the regiment, the Hun army, the nation that had taken Sam's life. Her resentment was against those who had come later, and whom she refused to dignify with the amicable name of Hun. She hated Hitler's war for diminishing the memory of the Great War, for allotting it a number, the mere first among two. And she hated the way in which the Great War was held responsible for its successor, as if Sam, Denis and all the East Lancashires who fell were partly the cause of that business. Sam had done what he could – he had served and died – and was punished all too quickly with becoming subservient in memory. Time did not behave rationally. Fifty years back to the Somme; a hundred beyond that to Waterloo; four hundred more to Agincourt, or Azincourt as the French preferred. Yet these distances had now been squeezed closer to one another. She blamed it on 1939–1945.

She knew to keep away from those parts of France where the second war happened, or at least where it was remembered. In the early years of the Morris, she had sometimes made the mistake of imagining herself on holiday, of being a tourist. She might thoughtlessly stop in a lay-by, or be taking a stroll down a back lane in some tranquil, heat-burdened part of the country, when a neat tablet inserted in a dry wall would assault her. It would commemorate Monsieur Un Tel, *lâchement assassiné par les Allemands*, or *tué*, or *fusillé*, and then an insulting modern date: 1943, 1944, 1945. They blocked the view, these deaths and these dates; they demanded attention by their recency. She refused, she refused.

When she stumbled like this upon the second war, she would hurry to the nearest village for consolation. She always knew where to look: next to the church, the *mairie*, the railway station; at a fork in the road; on a dusty square with cruelly pollarded limes and a few rusting café tables. There she would find her damp-stained memorial with its heroic *poilu*, grieving widow, triumphant Marianne, rowdy cockerel. Not that the story she read on the plinth needed any sculptural illustration. 67 against 9, 83 against 12, 40 against 5, 27 against 2: here was the eternal corroboration she sought, the historical corrigendum. She would touch the names cut into stone, their gilding washed away on the weather-side. Numbers whose familiar proportion declared the terrible primacy of the Great War. Her eye would check down the bigger list, snagging at a name repeated twice, thrice, four, five, six times: one male generation of an entire family taken away to known and honoured burial. In the bossy statistics of death she would find the comfort she needed.

She would spend the last night at Aix-Noulette (101 to 7); at Souchez (48 to 6), where she remembered Plouvier, Maxime, Sergent, killed on 17th December 1916, the last of his village to die before her Sam; at Carency (19 to 1); at Ablain-Saint-Nazaire (66 to 9), eight of whose male Lherbiers had died, four on the *champ d'honneur*, three as *victimes civiles*, one a *civil fusillé par l'ennemi*. Then, the next morning, cocked with grief, she would set off for Cabaret Rouge while dew was still on the grass. There was consolation in solitude and damp knees. She no longer talked to Sam; everything had been said decades ago. The heart had been expressed, the apologies made, the secrets given. She no longer wept, either; that too had stopped. But the hours she spent with him at Cabaret Rouge were the most vital of her life. They always had been.

The D937 did its reminding elbow at Cabaret Rouge, making sure you slowed out of respect, drawing your attention to Brigadier Sir Frank Higginson's handsome domed portico, which served as both entrance gate and memorial arch.

From the portico, the burial ground dropped away at first, then sloped up again towards the standing cross on which hung not Christ but a metal sword. Symmetrical, amphitheatrical, Cabaret Rouge held 6,676 British soldiers, sailors, Marines and airmen; 732 Canadians; 121 Australians; 42 South Africans; 7 New Zealanders; 2 members of the Royal Guernsey Light Infantry; 1 Indian; 1 member of an unknown unit; and 4 Germans.

It also contained, or more exactly had once had scattered over it, the ashes of Brigadier Sir Frank Higginson, Secretary to the Imperial War Graves Commission, who had died in 1958 at the age of sixty-eight. That showed true loyalty and remembrance. His widow, Lady Violet Lindsley Higginson, had died four years later, and her ashes had been scattered here too. Fortunate Lady Higginson. Why should the wife of a brigadier who, whatever he had done in the Great War, had not died, be allowed such enviable and meritorious burial, and yet the sister of one of those soldiers whom the fortune of war had led to known and honoured burial be denied such comfort? The Commission had twice denied her request, saying that a military cemetery did not receive civilian ashes. The third time she had written they had been less polite, referring her brusquely to their earlier correspondence.

There had been incidents down the years. They had stopped her coming for the eleventh hour of the eleventh day of the eleventh month by refusing her permission to sleep the night beside his grave. They said they did not have camping facilities; they affected to sympathize, but what if everybody else wanted to do the same? She replied that it was quite plain that no one else wanted to do the same but that if they did then such a desire should be respected. However, after some years she ceased to miss the official ceremony: it seemed to her full of people who remembered improperly, impurely.

There had been problems with the planting. The grass at the cemetery was French grass, and it seemed to her of the coarser type, inappropriate for British soldiers to lie beneath. Her campaign over this with the Commission led nowhere. So one spring she took out a small spade and a square yard of English turf kept damp in a plastic bag. After dark she dug out the offending French grass and relaid the softer English turf, patting it into place, then stamping it in. She was pleased with her work, and the next year, as she approached the grave, saw no indication of her mending. But when she knelt, she realized that her work had been undone: the French grass was back again.

The same had happened when she had surreptitiously planted her bulbs. Sam liked tulips, yellow ones especially, and one autumn she had pushed half a dozen bulbs into the earth. But the following spring, when she returned, there were only dusty geraniums in front of his stone.

There had also been the desecration. Not so very long ago. Arriving shortly after dawn, she found something on the grass which at first she put down to a dog. But when she saw the same in front of 1685 Private W. A. Andrade 4th Bn. London Regt. R. Fus. 15th March 1915, and in front of 675 Private Leon Emanuel Levy The Cameronians (Sco. Rif.) 16th August 1916 aged 21 And the Soul Returneth to God Who Gave It – Mother, she judged it most unlikely that a dog, or three dogs, had managed to find the only three Jewish graves in the cemetery. She gave the caretaker the rough edge of her tongue. He admitted that such desecration had occurred before, also that paint had been sprayed, but he always tried to arrive before anyone else and remove the signs. She told him that he might be honest but he was clearly idle. She blamed the second war. She tried not to think about it again.

For her, now, the view back to 1917 was uncluttered: the decades were mown grass, and at their end was a row of white headstones, domino-thin. 1358 Private Samuel M. Moss East Lancashire Regt. 21st January 1917, and in the middle the Star of David. Some graves in Cabaret Rouge were anonymous, with no identifying words or symbols; some had inscriptions, regimental badges, Irish harps, springboks, maple leaves, New Zealand ferns. Most had Christian crosses; only three displayed the Star of David. Private Andrade, Private Levy and Private Moss. A British soldier buried beneath the Star of

David: she kept her eyes on that. Sam had written from training camp that the fellows chaffed him, but he had always been Jewy Moss at school, and they were good fellows, most of them, as good inside the barracks as outside, anyway. They made the same remarks he'd heard before, but Jewy Moss was a British soldier, good enough to fight and die with his comrades, which is what he had done, and what he was remembered for. She pushed away the second war, which muddled things. He was a British soldier, East Lancashire Regiment, buried at Cabaret Rouge beneath the Star of David.

She wondered when they would plough them up, Herbécourt, Devonshire, Quarry, Blighty Valley, Ulster Tower, Thistle Dump and Caterpillar Valley; Maison Blanche and Cabaret Rouge. They said they never would. This land, she read everywhere, was 'the free gift of the

French people for the perpetual resting place of those of the allied armies who fell . . .' and so on. EVERMORE, they said, and she wanted to hear: for all future time. The War Graves Commission, her successive members of parliament, the Foreign Office, the commanding officer of Sammy's regiment, all told her the same. She didn't believe them. Soon — in fifty years or so — everyone who had served in the War would be dead; and at some point after that, everyone who had known anyone who had served would also be dead. What if memory-grafting did not work, or the memories themselves were deemed shameful? First, she guessed, those little stone tablets in the back lanes would be chiselled out, since the French and the Germans had officially stopped hating one another years ago, and it would not do for German tourists to be accused of the cowardly assassinations perpetrated by their ancestors. Then the war memorials would come down, with their important statistics. A few might be held to have architectural interest; but some new, cheerful generation would find them morbid, and dream up better things to enliven the villages. And after that it would be time to plough up the cemeteries, to put them back to good agricultural use: they had lain fallow for too long. Priests and politicians would make it all right, and the farmers would get their land back, fertilized with blood and bone. Thiepval might become a listed building, but would they keep Brigadier Sir Frank Higginson's domed portico? That elbow in the D937 would be declared a traffic hazard; all it needed was a drunken casualty for the road to be made straight again after all these years. Then the great forgetting could begin, the fading into the landscape. The war would be levelled to a couple of museums, a set of demonstration trenches, and a few names, shorthand for pointless sacrifice.

Might there be one last fiery glow of remembering? In her own case, it would not be long before her annual renewals ceased, before the clerical error of her life was corrected; yet even as she pronounced herself an antique, her memories seemed to sharpen. If this happened to the individual, could it not also happen on a national scale? Might there not be, at some point in the first decades of the twenty-first century, one final moment, lit by evening sun, before the whole thing was handed over to the archivists? Might there not be a great looking-back down the mown grass of the decades, might not a gap in the trees discover the curving ranks of slender headstones, white tablets holding up to the eye their bright names and terrifying dates, their harps and springboks, maple leaves and ferns, their

Christian crosses and their Stars of David? Then, in the space of a wet blink, the gap in the trees would close and the mown grass disappear, a violent indigo cloud would cover the sun, and history, gross history, daily history, would forget. Is this how it would be?

# READ MORE IN PENGUIN

For complete information about books available from Penguin and how to order them, please write to us at the appropriate address below. Please note that for copyright reasons the selection of books varies from country to country.

IN THE UNITED KINGDOM: Please write to *Dept. EP, Penguin Books Ltd, Bath Road, Harmondsworth, Middlesex UB7 0DA.*

IN THE UNITED STATES: Please write to *Consumer Sales, Penguin USA, P.O. Box 999, Dept. 17109, Bergenfield, New Jersey 07621-0120.* VISA and MasterCard holders call 1-800-253-6476 to order Penguin titles.

IN CANADA: Please write to *Penguin Books Canada Ltd, 10 Alcorn Avenue, Suite 300, Toronto, Ontario M4V 3B2.*

IN AUSTRALIA: Please write to *Penguin Books Australia Ltd, P.O. Box 257, Ringwood, Victoria 3134.*

IN NEW ZEALAND: Please write to *Penguin Books (NZ) Ltd, Private Bag 102902, North Shore Mail Centre, Auckland 10.*

IN INDIA: Please write to *Penguin Books India Pvt Ltd, 706 Eros Apartments, 56 Nehru Place, New Delhi 110 019.*

IN THE NETHERLANDS: Please write to *Penguin Books Netherlands bv, Postbus 3507, NL-1001 AH Amsterdam.*

IN GERMANY: Please write to *Penguin Books Deutschland GmbH, Metzlerstrasse 26, 60594 Frankfurt am Main.*

IN SPAIN: Please write to *Penguin Books S. A., Bravo Murillo 19, 1° B, 28015 Madrid.*

IN ITALY: Please write to *Penguin Italia s.r.l., Via Felice Casati 20, I-20124 Milano.*

IN FRANCE: Please write to *Penguin France S. A., 17 rue Lejeune, F-31000 Toulouse.*

IN JAPAN: Please write to *Penguin Books Japan, Ishikiribashi Building, 2-5-4, Suido, Bunkyo-ku, Tokyo 112.*

IN SOUTH AFRICA: Please write to *Longman Penguin Southern Africa (Pty) Ltd, Private Bag X08, Bertsham 2013.*